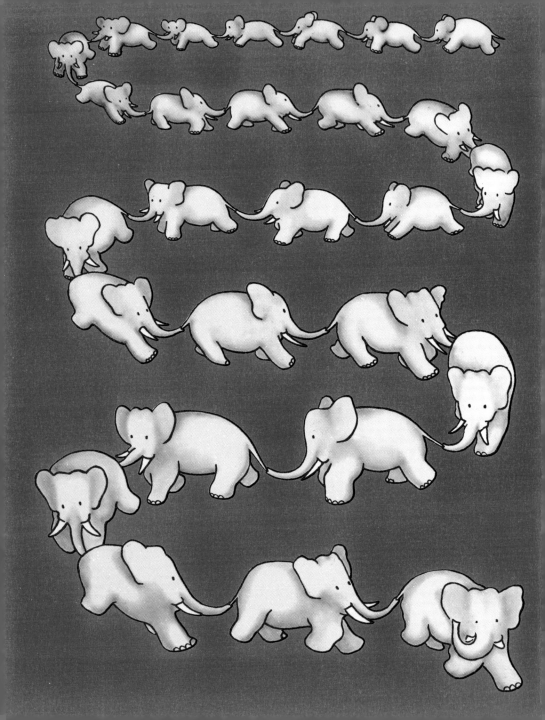

JEAN DE BRUNHOFF

BABAR

AND

FATHER CHRISTMAS

Translated from the French
by Merle Haas

Dragonfly Books · Alfred A. Knopf
New York

A DRAGONFLY BOOK PUBLISHED BY ALFRED A. KNOPF, INC.
Copyright 1940 by Random House, Inc.

All rights reserved under International and Pan-American Copyright
Conventions. Published in the United States by Alfred A. Knopf, Inc.,
New York, and simultaneously in Canada by Random House of Canada
Limited, Toronto. Distributed by Random House, Inc., New York.
Originally published by Random House, Inc., in 1940.

Library of Congress Cataloging-in-Publication Data

Brunhoff, Jean de, 1899–1937.
[Babar et le Père Noël. English]
Babar and Father Christmas / Jean de Brunhoff ; translated from
the French by Merle Haas.
p.   cm.
"Dragonfly books."
Summary: Babar, the King of the Elephants, sets out to find Father
Christmas and bring him back to visit the children of elephant
country.
ISBN 0-679-80698-9 (pbk.)
[1. Elephants—Fiction.   2. Santa Claus—Fiction.   3. Christmas—
Fiction.]   I. Title.
PZ7.B828428Bab   1990
[E]—dc20   90-30391   CIP   AC

First Dragonfly edition: October 1990

Manufactured in the United States of America
10 9 8 7 6 5 4 3 2

One day Zéphir calls to his friends
Arthur, Pom, Flora and Alexander:
"Listen, listen to this wonderful tale which I've just heard!
It seems that in Man's country,
every year, on the night before Christmas,
a very kind old gentleman with a large white beard,
wearing a red suit with a pointed hood,
flies over the countryside.
He carries with him great quantities of toys
and gives them to the little children.
They call him Father Christmas.
It is difficult to catch a glimpse of him
for he comes down the chimney while one sleeps.
Next morning the children know he has been there
because they find toys in their shoes.
Why shouldn't we write to him and ask him to come
here too and see us in the Elephants' country?"

"Three cheers! What a fine idea!" says Alexander.
"But what shall we say in the letter?" asks Arthur. "We must write and
tell Father Christmas what we would like him to bring us," suggests Pom.
"Let's consider very carefully before we write," adds Flora.
They remain quiet a moment and think it over.

Zéphir decides a bicycle would be just what he wants,
Flora would love to have a doll.
Alexander wants a butterfly net,
Pom a big bag of candies and a little Teddy Bear.
As for Arthur, his dream is to have a train.

Then, each having decided what to wish for,
Zéphir is chosen to write the letter,
for he has the best handwriting.
He applies himself to his task.
Arthur remembers that a stamp must be put on the envelope.
Then they each sign their names and go off together
in great glee to mail the letter.

Every morning the five friends eagerly await the postman.
They rush out to meet him as soon as they see him coming.
But alas, although the postman searches carefully,
there is no answer from Father Christmas.
One day Babar happens to see them and says to himself:
"Whatever can be the matter with those children?
They look so dreadfully sad."

So he calls to them
and says:
"Come on, tell me
what's the matter".
Zéphir tells him the story of his letter.
"And you haven't had an answer? Is that it?" asks Babar.
"You must have forgotten to put a stamp on it."
"Oh no we didn't, Arthur remembered to."
"Well, then Father Christmas hasn't had time to answer it yet.
Cheer up and run along now and play.
Possibly you've given me a very excellent idea."
Babar pulls out his pipe and smokes.
He paces thoughtfully up and down, lost in thought.
"I wonder why I never thought myself
of asking
Father Christmas
to come to the
Elephants' country."

"The best thing to do would be to start out at once to find him. If I ask him personally he will surely not refuse to come."

His mind made up, Babar hurries to inform Celeste of his intentions. She helps him to pack and get ready.

She would like very much to go along, but Babar explains to her that she'll be needed at home to rule the country during his absence, and also remarks that queer characters like Father Christmas are often shy, and rarely allow themselves to be approached by more than one person at a time.

Babar arrives in Europe after a very good journey. He has just stepped from the train. In order not to be recognized he has left his crown at home.

HÔTEL DU COQ ROUGE

He drives to a little old hotel which is clean and quiet,
and is given a room which pleases him.
Next he undresses and washes up a bit.
One always feels so refreshed after a good cleaning up.
"What can be making that funny little noise?"
wonders Babar as he dries himself off.
Without moving he looks around,
and all of a sudden he sees three young mice.
The least timid of them says:
"Good-day, my stout Sir,

Are we to have the pleasure of your company for long?"
"Oh no, I'm just passing through.
I'm looking for Father Christmas," answers Babar.
"You're looking for Father Christmas.--
Why, goodness, he's here in this very house, we know him well.
We'll show you his room," chorused the three little mice.
"How wonderful! What really extraordinary luck!
Just give me time to put on my dressing gown,
and I'll be with you,"
cries the excited Babar.

"But where on earth
are these little mice leading me?" wonders Babar
as he stops a moment
on the stairs to catch his breath.
"Father Christmas must live
way up on the top floor.
No doubt he likes to have a good view
and plenty of open space around him."
While Babar is making these observations,
the three little mice reach the attic.
Whatever are they doing over there in that corner?
They seem all excited! "Where are you?" calls Babar.
"Up here in the attic," answer the little mice.
"Come quickly! We have taken Father Christmas
down from the top of the tree."

When Babar joins them,
the delighted little mice say:
"There is Father Christmas!
He lives here peacefully
the whole year round,
excepting on Christmas Day
when they come and fetch him
to hang on top of a new Christmas tree.
After the holiday he resumes his place
in this corner
and we can come and play with him again."
"But this isn't the one I'm looking for,
I want to find the real live Father Christmas,
not a doll!"
says Babar sadly.

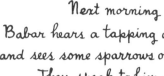
Next morning
Babar hears a tapping at his window,
and sees some sparrows outside on the sill.
They speak to him and say:
"We understand that you are searching
for the real live Father Christmas.
We know him well
and are going to take you to him."
And off they fly joyously.
Pointing out the way to Babar,
they lead him across the big bridge over the river.
"We're almost there," they call.
"We usually find him around here,
he sleeps under the bridges."
"Well, well, that is strange," thinks Babar.
"There he is! There he is!" cry all the little sparrows
together. "He's over there next to that fisherman
casting his line."

Babar, still a bit astonished
at this old fellow's odd appearance,
greets him and says:
"Excuse me, Sir.
But are you really
the true Father Christmas,
the one who brings toys
to all the children?"
"Alas no," answers the old man.
"My name is Lazzaro Campeotti.
I am an artist's model
and my friends the artists
have nicknamed me
Father Christmas.
Now everybody calls me by that name."
Very much disappointed,
Babar strolls thoughtfully
along the river banks.

Stopping at one of the book stalls,
Babar finds a book with
pictures of Father Christmas.
He quickly buys it and takes it
back to his room to examine it
more carefully.
Unfortunately the text is written
in a language which
he does not understand. He goes down to explain his
difficulty to the hotel manager, who helpfully gives him
the address of a professor at the school where his son
is studying. "Mr. Gillianez will surely be able to
translate your book," says he.
Without losing a moment, Babar is at the door
of Professor Gillianez' house ringing the bell. He finds
him at home but after a glance at the book the Professor says
that to his great regret he is unable to read it either. He gives Babar

the address of the famous
Professor William Jones.
An hour later
Babar is in
this man's study.
The Professor carefully
examines the book,
and shakes his head gloomily.
Finally he turns to Babar who has been
waiting patiently, and says:
"Your book is very difficult to read.
It is written in old style Gothic letters.
There are facts in it about the life of Father Christmas,
and they say he lives in Bohemia,
not far from the little town of PRJMNESWE.
But I do not find any more
definite information on this point."

Babar goes off and sits on a bench in the public park
to think the matter over.
The birds recognize him and come over to inquire
whether he has found Father Christmas.
"No, not yet," answers Babar. "I only know that he lives
far away from here near the town of PRJMNESWE. Truly this
is a difficult search." Just then a little dog who is passing
by says to Babar: "Pardon me, Sir. I'm very good at finding things
which are lost, because I have a highly developed sense of smell.

If only I could have a sniff of that doll,
which Father Christmas gave to little Virginia over there,
I'm sure I'd be able to help you find him.
I would be very glad to go with you
because I am a little homeless dog."
Upon hearing these words
Babar looks at the dog and says:
"Agreed. I'll take you along with me."
Then off he goes to buy a beautiful new doll
for Virginia which she gladly accepts
in exchange for her other one.
Babar
lets the dog
sniff the
old doll,
and feeds him
a piece of
candy.

Before starting out Babar goes back
to see the learned Professor William Jones
who returns his book
and gives him a few additional directions.
Father Christmas apparently lives
in a forest on a mountain
about twelve miles from PRJMNESWE.
Babar arrives at the little town
after a difficult journey.

It is very cold and a great deal of
snow has fallen.
Babar therefore equips
himself accordingly.
He buys some skiis,
hires a sleigh and has himself
driven to the foot of the mountain.
Pretty soon he has to get out and,
accompanied only by his faithful Duck,
(this is the name he has given his dog)
he starts to climb in the direction
of the mysterious forest,
skiis on his feet, and a
heavily laden pack on his back.
Duck is very much excited. He sniffs
here and there and yaps softly.
Now he stands still, his tail lifted,
his nose twitching hard. He must have
caught the scent of Father Christmas.

Suddenly
Duck is
off on
the run.
"I've got it!
I've got it!
We're on
the right track."
His loud
barking echoes
through
the woods.
But what
is that
stirring
in this
wild forest?

It is a band of little mountain dwarfs
who have hidden themselves behind the tree trunks.
Duck would like to see them nearer by,
but they rush at him pelting him fast and furiously
with
hard-packed
snowballs
which land
on his head,
in his eyes
and on
his sides.

_26_

. Half choked,
half blinded,
his tail
between his legs,
Duck decides
to retreat.
He quickly
runs to rejoin
his master,
and arrives
breathless,
feeling very
foolish.
When Babar
sees him
he stops short
and asks:

"What's happened?" Duck then tells him of his
adventure with the little bearded dwarfs.
"Good, we must be getting nearer," replies Babar.
"I am
very eager
to meet
those dwarfs,
lead me
to
them."

A few minutes later
it is Babar's turn
to meet the dwarfs.
They try to frighten him too,
and rush bravely towards him, and pelt him,
but Babar calmly takes a deep breath
and blows it out hard in their direction.
They all tumble down one on top of the other,
and as soon as they can scramble back to their feet,
off they run and noiselessly disappear.
Babar roars with laughter,
and continues on his way, following Duck
who has now found the scent again.

The little dwarfs have run
to find Father Christmas
and they tell him, all jabbering at once,
that an enormous animal
with a long nose
blew on them so hard that he knocked them down
and chased them away.
Father Christmas listens attentively.
The little dwarfs add that when they fled,
this big monster was quite near,
and that, guided
by an ugly little cur,
he was heading straight for the secret cave
of Father Christmas.

They were right. Babar is nearing the cave,
but a storm of extraordinary violence suddenly bursts upon him.
The wind blows so hard
that the snow-flakes prick his eyes and skin.
It is impossible to see. Babar struggles desperately;
then, realizing the danger of obstinately forging ahead blindly,
he decides to dig himself a hole for shelter.

Then he rigs up a roof with his skiis and ski-poles and some snow
blocks. The two companions are fairly well protected now.
"Whew! It is cold and my trunk is beginning to freeze,"
thinks Babar. Duck also is cold and tired.
All of a sudden, Babar feels the earth giving away under him,
and he and Duck drop out of sight.
Where have they fallen?

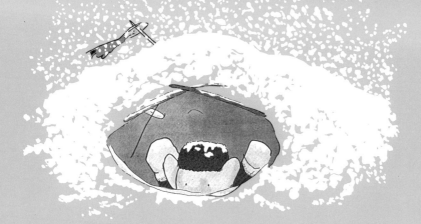

Without realizing it they have dropped right down through a chimney vent into the cave of Father Christmas. "Father Christmas!" cries the amazed Babar. "Duck, we've arrived at our destination." Whereupon he faints, worn out with fatigue, the cold and the excitement. "Quick, little mountain dwarfs, forget your quarrel, we must undress him and get him warm," says Father Christmas.

They all set to immediately. They undress him, and give him a
good alcohol rub, working over him energetically with big brushes.
The dwarf chemist gives him some brandy.
Then finally, Babar drinks a fine bowl of hot soup
with Father Christmas
and thanks him from the bottom of his heart.

While Father Christmas shows him around, Babar explains that he has
made this long journey to ask him to visit the Elephants' country.

N.B.- This tour includes the big room in which Father Christmas usually lives; the room into
which Babar fell through the hole, which one can see in the upper right hand corner; and
the toy rooms, the doll room, the tin soldier room, the armory with toy guns, the room full

Won't he distribute toys to the elephant children, just as he does to the children of men? Father Christmas is much touched by this request,

of trains, the room with building blocks, the room where the stuffed animals are kept, the one with tennis racquets and balls, etc...(all these things neatly packed in boxes and in bags.) And then they visited the dwarfs' dormitories, the elevators worked by pulleys and the machine shop.

but he tells Babar that he will not be able to visit
the Elephants' country Christmas night
because he is very tired.
He adds: "I had great difficulty last year
in completing the usual delivery and distribution of toys
to the children all over the world."
"Oh, Father Christmas, I understand perfectly,"
says Babar, "but if this is the

case you must take care of yourself. Why not live on the earth's surface for a while and leave your underground home? Come back with me now to our country and bask in the sun.

You will be rested and cured for Christmas."

Charmed by this suggestion, Father Christmas instructs the little dwarfs to keep an eye on everything for him.

Then off he goes in his flying machine, F.C. No 1, accompanied by Babar and Duck.

Here they are in the Elephants' country. Father Christmas admires the countryside and is quickly surrounded by the elephants who rush over to bid him welcome. Pom, Flora and Alexander hurry over too. In order to get the best view, Arthur has climbed to the roof of a house and Zéphir is up in a tree. When the excitement quiets down Queen Celeste introduces her three children and Arthur and Zéphir to Father Christmas. "Oh, you are the ones who wrote me", he says, "I am delighted to meet you and I promise you a Merry Christmas."

Father Christmas
    often goes
    out riding
on zebra back.
Babar rides
    along on
his bicycle.
    And

Father Christmas takes a sun-bath for two full hours
    every day, following Dr. Capoulosse's instructions.
        Sometimes, Pom, Flora and Alexander
        come to watch him as he lies in his hammock,
        but they are careful to make no noise,
            so as not to disturb him.

One day
Father Christmas
says to Babar:
"My dear friend,
thank you very much
for all that you
have done for me.

Christmas is nearly here and I must leave to distribute the
awaited gifts to the children of men.
But I'm not forgetting the promise
I made to the little elephants.
Can you guess what I have in this bag?
A real Santa Claus suit made to your measure!
It is a magic suit which will enable you
to fly through the air,
and your bag will always be full of toys.
You can take my place here Christmas eve.
I promise you I'll return when my work is done
and I'll bring the children a fine
Christmas tree."

On the night before Christmas Babar follows out these instructions.
As soon as he puts on the suit and beard, he notices that he instantly
becomes lighter and is at the same time able to fly with ease.
"This is really extraordinary! And what a good way to distribute
all the gifts to the children!" thinks Babar.

He hurries in order to get through with his task before dawn.
What joy there will be in every house on Christmas morning
when the little elephants awake!
In the royal palace Queen Celeste peeks through the door of the
children's room. Pom is emptying his stocking, Flora is rocking
her doll, and Alexander is jumping up and down on his bed,
exclaiming: "What a wonderful Christmas!
What a wonderful Christmas!"

As he had promised, Father Christmas has come back bringing them a beautiful Christmas tree. And thanks to him the family celebration is a great success.

Arthur, Zéphir, Pom, Flora and Alexander
have never seen anything as beautiful as
this fir tree all shining with lights.

Next day,
Father Christmas flies away again
in his airplane
to rejoin his little subjects, the dwarfs,
in his underground palace.
On the banks of the big lake,
Babar, Celeste, Arthur, Zéphir,
and the three children
sadly wave their handkerchiefs.
Fortunately,
Father Christmas has promised
to come back
to the Elephants' country
every year.

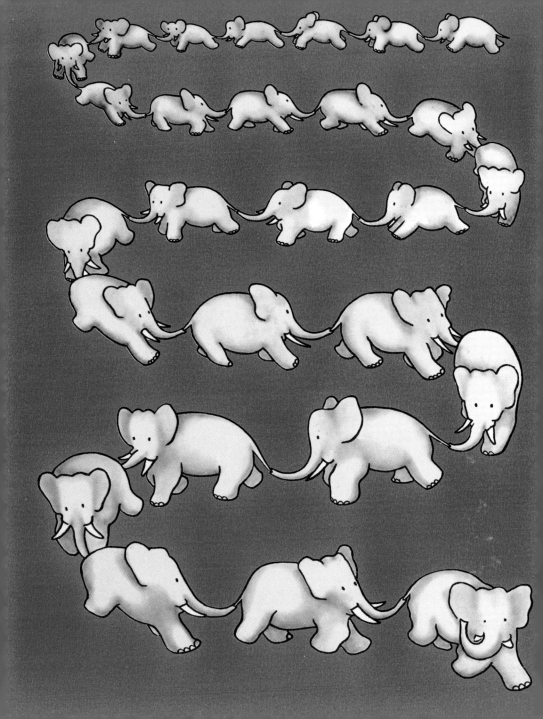

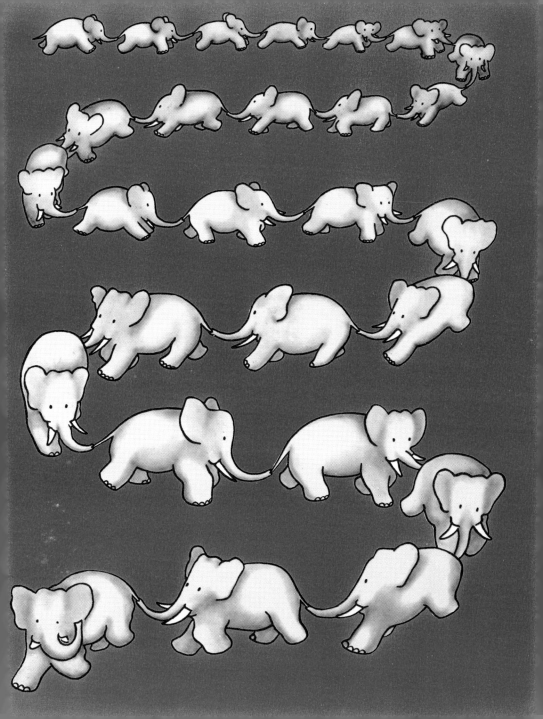